This Humphrey book belongs to

Humphrey's

Christmas

Sally Hunter

PUFFIN BOOKS

Humphrey and Lottie love
Christmastime . . .

watching the soft, floaty snow

. . . running really fast . . .

... Ooops!

...being Daddy's little helper...

. . . trying to be very
still and quiet . . .

... making pretty decorations

and hanging them on their
very own tree . . .

. . . watching Mummy cooking

...yummy!

then helping with the best bits!

But most exciting of all...

is the last bedtime

before Christmas Day.

Lottie draws a lovely letter
for Father Christmas...

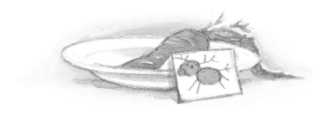

...remembers to leave a
treat for Rudolph.

Sssh now!... No more silly billies...off to sleep +

Then she puts her babies to bed.

Mummy reads a special story
all about Baby Jesus

and has an extra long cuddle.

Night, night, little Humphrey.

x

Happy Christmas.

"Hold on tight, Mop!" "Aaah! Choo choo

Ooh! You're lovely! You can be Lulu's Best Friend!"

For Paul ♡
Love
Your Sal
x

PUFFIN BOOKS

Published by the Penguin Group:
London, New York, Australia, Canada, India, New Zealand and South Africa
Penguin Books Ltd, Registered Offices: 80 Strand, London WC2R ORL, England

www.penguin.com

First published by Viking 2001
Published in Puffin Books 2002
1 3 5 7 9 10 8 6 4 2

Printed in Singapore

ISBN 0−140−56884−0

To find out more about Humphrey's world, visit the web site at:
www.humphreys-corner.com